WYDALE D GILCHRIST

Secrets SURPRISES *in* LATE NIGHTS

Published by:
D'Lamont Intimate Ideas LLC
Michigan, United States

ISBN: 979-8-9929652-4-7 (Paperback)

First paperback edition 2025

Printed in the United States of America

Table of Contents

The Celebration Before The Storm

It was Friday evening around 8 p.m. when three best friends decided to meet up for dinner. Liz, excited about her recent promotion, had called everyone to share the news. Mike, Liz's best friend, beamed, "Congrats, boo!" His boyfriend, William, was on his way to join them, and Mike asked him to pick up a caramel apple ice cream cake he'd pre-ordered to celebrate Liz's achievement.

As Mike excused himself to use the restroom, he spotted Sue and Kevin at the host table. "We're over there," Mike said, pointing them toward the group. Sue and Kevin made their way to the table, and as Sue approached, Liz exclaimed, "Damn, bitch! Where is the rest of your clothes?" Everyone burst out laughing as Sue hugged Liz and kissed her on the cheek.

When Mike and William returned, William was wearing a tight shirt and short shorts with a ripped back pocket. Kevin shot William a bewildered look, as though he had just stepped out of a circus. Mike ignored the side-eyes, stood up, and raised his glass. "Let's toast to my best friend

Liz and her big promotion!" Everyone cheered, clinking glasses and shouting, "Congratulations, Liz, bitch!"

Liz thanked her friends but seemed visibly upset. Mike noticed and pulled her aside. "What's wrong, boo?" he asked gently. Liz burst into tears, burying her face in his chest. "I'm not going to ask again—what's going on?" Mike pressed. Between sobs, Liz muttered, "Fuck her," over and over.

Realizing Liz needed space, Mike guided her back to the table and announced, "She's done for the night." The group quickly wrapped things up, gathered their things, and headed out. Sue hugged Liz on the way out and paused to admire a shiny red 2026

Mercedes Benz parked in a handicapped spot. "Girl, I wish that was mine," Sue joked. Liz laughed, "Me too."

As they walked to Sue's car, Liz's phone rang. It was her girlfriend, Tree, who shouted, "Hold up, you need to walk toward Mike's car right now!" Liz, confused, followed Tree's instructions. A pair of hands suddenly covered her eyes, and she felt a playful bite on her neck. She spun around to find Tree grinning.

Liz jumped into Tree's arms like a kid and screamed, "I love you so much!" Tree handed Liz a pair of keys and instructed her to press the unlock button. When the Mercedes-Benzes lights flashed, Liz screamed, "No way, baby!"

Mike yelled from across the lot, "Bitch, that's cute! What are you going to name her?" Liz laughed, still in shock, as Tree ushered her into the car.

On the drive home, Tree teased, "There's one more surprise waiting." Liz, both nervous and excited, glanced at Tree but didn't press for details. When they pulled into the driveway, Tree blindfolded Liz and led her into the house.

Tree poured two glasses of wine and brought out chocolate-covered strawberries. The night turned passionate as the two explored their intimacy, with Liz reveling in Tree's thoughtful gestures and affection.

Tree entered the bedroom carrying two glasses of wine and a tray of chocolate-covered strawberries. She set them down gently on the nightstand, her eyes locked on Liz, who was now dressed in the red lingerie Tree had laid out. Liz sat at the edge of the bed; her curves complimented perfectly by the delicate lace.

Tree leaned in, her lips brushing Liz's ear as she whispered, "You're the sexiest woman alive." Liz's breath hitched as Tree kissed her neck, each touch of her lips sending shivers down her spine.

Tree's hands trailed down Liz's sides, her fingers grazing the soft fabric of the lingerie. She kissed her way down Liz's chest, slowly peeling the straps from her shoulders. As the lingerie slid down, Tree circled Liz's nipples with her tongue, teasing them until they hardened under her touch.

Liz let out a soft moan, her hands tangling in Tree's dreads as her body arched in response. Tree moved lower, kissing every inch of Liz's stomach while her hands explored Liz's thighs, gently spreading them apart.

Tree grabbed a chocolate-covered strawberry and traced it along Liz's inner thigh, the sweet juice leaving a sticky trail on her skin. She paused, letting the strawberry rest against Liz's lips before licking it away with her tongue. Liz gasped, her hips lifting in anticipation as Tree's tongue dipped lower.

Tree kissed her way down to Liz's center, her tongue gliding over her wet folds, savoring the taste. Liz cried out, her body trembling as Tree flicked her tongue against her clit, slow and deliberate. "Oh my God, baby," Liz moaned, gripping the sheets as Tree's tongue worked her in ways that made her entire body quiver.

Sliding two fingers inside Liz, Tree found her rhythm, curling her fingers just right to hit that perfect spot. Liz's moans grew louder, her body writhing as Tree increased her pace, her tongue circling Liz's clit in perfect harmony with her fingers.

"I'm so close," Liz whimpered, her voice shaky. Tree smirked and leaned up for a moment, locking eyes with Liz. "I'm not done with you yet," she teased, sliding her fingers out and replacing them with the vibrating rabbit toy.

Liz nearly screamed as Tree turned it on, thrusting it deep inside her while her tongue continued to lavish attention on her swollen clit. Her body shook uncontrollably, her climax hitting her like a wave. Liz's legs clamped around Tree's head, pulling her closer as her entire body trembled in ecstasy.

But Tree wasn't finished. She climbed onto the bed, grabbing Liz by the waist and flipping her over. Liz grinned, her confidence returning as she reached into the nightstand, pulling out her sleek black strap-on. She strapped it on, the shiny surface glinting in the dim bedroom light.

Liz stood behind Tree, who was on all fours, her body glistening with sweat. Liz spread Tree's cheeks, teasing her with the tip of the strap before thrusting it inside in one smooth motion. Tree moaned loudly, her back arching as Liz grabbed her dreads for leverage.

"Harder," Tree begged, her voice hoarse with desire. Liz obliged, pounding into her with deep, steady strokes that left Tree gasping for air. Liz leaned over, her breasts pressing against Tree's back as she whispered, "You feel so good, baby."

Tree's hands gripped the sheets tightly, her body rocking in time with Liz's thrusts. Liz reached around, her fingers finding

Tree's clit and rubbing it in quick, tight circles. Tree's moans turned into screams, her body shaking as she came hard, her juices soaking the strap.

Both women collapsed onto the bed, their bodies tangled together. Tree kissed Liz's forehead, still catching her breath. "You always know how to spoil me," Liz teased with a grin. Tree laughed softly, pulling Liz close. "Only because you deserve it."

They drifted off to sleep, their bodies still humming with the afterglow of their passion.

****

Saturday Morning Drama

Liz's peaceful morning was interrupted by Mike's frantic call. "Nigga, let me go!" he shouted through the phone. Liz groaned, trying to calm him down. "What's going on?" she asked. Mike explained that William had been coming home late, showering as soon as he arrived, and acting very suspicious.

The two were shouting, calling each other names. The argument escalated when Mike slapped William, who then retaliated by choking Mike until he turned blue. Mike fought back by twisting William's groin until he let go.

Liz promised to come over to help, and when she arrived with Tree, the tension between Mike and William was so thick it could be sliced with a knife.

A loud knock at the door startled everyone. Liz and Tree entered, worried about Mike's disheveled appearance. As Tree confronted William, his phone rang. Tree snatched it, answering sharply, "Who is this?" A deep voice replied, "Hey, baby you still coming over?" Tree handed the phone to Mike, who froze in disbelief.

After the mysterious call, William stormed out of the house, and Mike, overcome with emotion, drove to a nearby store. There, he ran into Sue, who sensed something was wrong. They agreed to meet for lunch to vent about their problems.

Meanwhile back at home, Mike decided to move William's belongings to the basement and left him a note: "Your new room is downstairs." Exhausted, Mike showered and collapsed into bed, determined to figure things out later.

****

Tangled Hearts, Twisted Lies

William crept into the house at 4:30 AM, carefully closing the door behind him. He tiptoed to the bedroom and saw Mike passed out, sprawled across the bed. Standing in the doorway, he sighed, shaking his head at the sight. Quietly, he gathered his clothes and made his way down to the basement. There, he found a note taped to the wall: "your new room is downstairs" William went outside to grab a bouquet of flowers, a bottle of gold Moët, and two basketball tickets from his car.

He placed them on the trunk so Mike would see them when he woke up, hoping they'd soften the blow. Wrapping himself in a blanket, William crashed on the living room couch, his heart heavy with guilt.

By 11:30 am, Mike was awake. Groggy, he texted Sue: "meet me at the steakhouse for happy hour." As he got out of bed, he spotted the gifts left by William. A smile began to blossom on his face, but the realization of betrayal quickly clouded his thoughts. Determined to act as if nothing were wrong, he got dressed, grabbed his keys, and headed for the door, ignoring William's sleeping figure on the couch.

At the steakhouse, Sue greeted Mike with a hug and an all-too-eager grin. "Girl," she said excitedly, sliding her phone across the table, "I have some dog-ass tea for you."

Mike's heart sank as he saw the image of William and Kevin, entangled in bed in a cheap hotel room. His stomach churned as Sue detailed how she got the photo from Kevin's phone.

"It's time we set these fools up," Sue said maliciously.

Mike nodded; his jaw tight. "Let's do it," he said, though his voice wavered slightly filled with hurt.

As the two schemed over appetizers, Sue revealed a secret of her own. She had been seeing Kevin behind her husband's back for months. "Oh, honey, if William wants to play dirty, let's just say Kevin taught me the game."

Mike's phone buzzed—it was William. "Did you like the gifts?" William asked hesitantly.

"They were...nice," Mike replied coldly, glancing at Sue, who mouthed, "play it cool."

Back at the house, William had cleaned up and prepared a romantic dinner. When Mike returned, William greeted him at the door with a passionate kiss. "I missed you so much," he murmured, trying to erase the tension between them.

But Mike, haunted by the image of William and Kevin, pushed William back gently. "Is this what you really want?" he asked, searching William's face for answers.

"Of course, baby," William replied earnestly.

Mike decided to confront him indirectly. He seduced William, leading him to their bedroom and whispering sweet nothings. But even as they shared an intense night together, Mike's mind raced with plans for his next move.

The next morning, Sue's plan kicked into action. She sent an anonymous text to Kevin, using

William's phone: "Meet me at the Grand Regency Hotel, Section J, tonight at 7 PM."

Meanwhile, Sue secretly invited Mike, Liz, and a few other key players to the hotel that evening.

Kevin arrived first, looking nervous as he sat in Section J. William arrived moments later, confused but hopeful that Kevin had called him there to sort things out.

As they exchanged awkward pleasantries, Mike and Sue stormed into the room, followed by Liz. "Caught in the act!" Sue yelled, throwing a glass of red wine at Kevin.

Mike slammed a folder onto the table. "I come with receipts!" he declared, pulling out screenshots of texts, hotel bills, and photos. Kevin and William sat stunned, unable to respond.

Sue leaned in close to Kevin. "You thought you could cheat on me and I wouldn't find out?

Well, guess what? I've been sleeping with someone else, too."

Kevin's face darkened with rage. "What are you talking about?" he asked, his voice trembling.

"I've been seeing Liz!" Sue announced, laughing cruelly.

The room erupted into chaos. Kevin tried to lunge at Sue, but Mike held him back. Liz, who had been silent until now, stepped forward and dropped another bombshell: "Oh, by the way, Sue isn't the only one cheating. Kevin, I've been seeing Tree."

Kevin's jaw dropped. "Tree?!"

"You know, your coworker." Liz smirked, clearly enjoying the drama.

The night spiraled further out of control. Tree arrived at the hotel after receiving an anonymous tip from Sue and was met with accusations from both Liz and Kevin. In the midst of it all, hotel security was called to break up the scene, but not before Sue slapped Kevin with divorce papers.

Back at their respective homes, tensions reached a boiling point. Kevin, in a fit of rage, set fire to the house he once shared with Sue. Meanwhile, Liz, heartbroken and furious, attacked Tree in a jealous rage, resulting in both of them being hospitalized.

****

The Aftermath

Months later, the fallout from the chaos continued to ripple through their lives.

Sue, now living with Liz as she awaited her funds from the insurance policy, began rebuilding her life as a single woman, focusing on her career.

A few months later, one early morning, Sue was at home getting ready for work. She brewed herself a strong black coffee with a single cube of sugar. She had recently started a job at a newspaper company, editing articles as they came in. Just as she was about to leave the house, her phone rang. It was her boss, asking her to come in later.

After hanging up, Sue dialed Liz.

"Hello, working woman!" Liz greeted cheerfully.

Sue smiled. "Hey, what's up, my girl? Where are you at?"

"I'm home, dressed, and ready to head out, but work told me to come in late," Liz replied.

"Say less," Sue said. "I'll be there in a sec. I just need to grab a few things. I'm pulling up."

Sue arrived at Liz's house shortly after. Liz handed her a cup of coffee. "Where have you been?" she teased.

Sue smirked mischievously. "Girl, last I checked, I was single. You need a little action, though— it's been months."

Liz chuckled. "I know it's been a while, but I just haven't found anyone since Tree and I broke up. Plus, I'm not even looking. I just want to have fun."

Sue handed Liz an envelope full of cash. "Thank you for letting me live with you," she said gratefully.

"Girl, anytime," Liz said with a warm smile. "We're sisters."

Sue headed out to her car, but before starting it, she received an unexpected call from a rehabilitation center. It was Kevin.

She answered, "Yes, I'll accept the collect call. Hey, Kevin. You still haven't signed the divorce papers I sent you."

Kevin sighed. "Sue, I've been in here for months. I was wrong, and I'll sign the papers. I also want to apologize for everything."

"That's all I wanted—a genuine apology," Sue replied, her voice softening. "I'm moving on now."

After hanging up, Sue sat in the car, overwhelmed by emotion. Tears streamed down her face, so she called Liz for support. Liz offered her some comforting advice, and Sue felt better after their conversation.

Later, Liz decided to call Tree. However, another woman answered the phone.

"This isn't Tree! Where's Tree?" Liz snapped.

Tree grabbed the phone. "Hello? What do you want, Liz?"

Liz scoffed. "I see you've already got someone else answering your phone. I just called for an apology for how you treated me." "Wow," Tree said, sounding surprised. "Well, I'm sorry. Bye." Frustrated, Liz hung up and headed to the patio to do yoga and meditate. She focused on releasing all the bad energy in her life. After her session, she sashayed around the house in her silk robe, blasting music, and preparing a hot bubble bath. She removed her makeup, shaved her legs, and relaxed in the tub.

As she scrolled through Facebook, she came across an old classmate, Tony, and sent him a friend request. He quickly accepted and messaged her.

"Hello, beautiful. What made you add me?"

Liz replied, "I like what I see."

The two exchanged compliments, and Tony asked Liz on a date.

"I don't know you like that," Liz responded.

"Well, let's fix that," Tony said.

Liz laughed. "Actually, I do know you. You went to Jackson State University with me."

Tony confessed, "I had a crush on you for three years, but you were in a relationship."

Liz responded playfully, "That's old news. Say less—meet me at JJ's Soul Bar and Grill at 8 PM."

Tony replied with excitement, "See you there!"

That evening, Liz looked stunning in a navy-blue outfit with gold Versace heels, her long Bohemian curls cascading down her back. Sue gasped when she saw her.

"Girl, you're sexy as hell! That man isn't going to keep his hands off you."

Liz laughed. "Pray for me. It's been years since I've been with a man!"

Liz arrived at JJ's Soul Bar and Grill, where Tony was waiting by valet. He opened her car door and said, "Welcome to my restaurant. Ready for a good time?"

Liz smiled. "I hope the food is as good as the service!"

Inside, the glittering gold interior took her breath away. Tony pulled out her chair, and Liz complimented his manners.

As they enjoyed the house special, Tony revealed he co-owned the restaurant with his family.

Liz was impressed and joked, "So you're really the head guy in charge?"

Tony chuckled. "You could say that."

As the night progressed, Tony asked, "Have you ever been dominant in a relationship?"

Liz hesitated. "I haven't been with a man in over 15 years. I'm just stepping out of my comfort zone, but I'd be open to trying new things."

Sensing her unease, Tony reassured her. "Are you okay?"

Liz smiled nervously. "I'm fine. You just caught me off guard."

After dinner, Tony offered a nightcap, but Liz politely declined, saying, "I have work in the morning."

As she drove home, Liz couldn't help but reflect on how much her life had changed.

Around 10:30 p.m., Liz called Sue.

"Did you enjoy your night?" Sue asked.

"Girl, yes!" Liz exclaimed. "Come to find out, he owns JJ's Soul Bar and Grill."

Sue gasped. "Omg! They've got some good ass chicken," she said, chuckling.

Liz hesitated before asking, "Do you think I should go over to Tony's for the night?"

"Hell yeah, you should," Sue replied without missing a beat. "Go get you some dick you never had before."

Liz laughed, hanging up the phone. Her heart raced as she dialed Tony's number.

Tony answered on the second ring. "I guess you changed your mind," he teased.

"I did!" Liz said excitedly. "Send me your address—I'll be right over."

As soon as Tony hung up, he jumped in the shower. Anticipation buzzed through him as he got ready, pulling out whips, chains, leather outfits, and other accessories. He turned on some slow jams to set the mood.

When a knock finally came at the door, Tony opened it to find Liz standing there, her face a mix of curiosity and shock.

Tony stood in the doorway wearing a black leather harness, his skin glistening with oil. He gave her a sly grin and held out a matching leather outfit. "Put this on," he said, leading her inside.

Liz followed him, her nerves bubbling as he escorted her into his bedroom. Her eyes widened when she saw a sex swing hanging in the center of the room.

"Tony," Liz said nervously, "you know I'm a virgin. I've never been with a man before. I told you that at dinner, remember?"

Tony turned to her, his expression soft but playful. "And you remember I told you I love to be dominated. That's what I want tonight."

He handed Liz a whip and dropped to his hands and knees. "I've been a bad boy," he said with a mischievous glint in his eye.

Liz took a deep breath, gripping the whip tightly. She swung it across his backside, finding confidence in his eager response.

"Yes! You've been a very bad boy," she said, her voice steady now. She walked over to his chest of toys and picked up a black, glittery nine-inch strap-on harness. Fixing it securely, she ordered, "Suck it."

Tony leaned forward, taking the strap into his mouth as Liz gripped the back of his head and pushed it deeper. She watched as he eagerly obeyed, then swung the whip across his back again, harder this time.

"Lay on the fucking bed!" she commanded.

Tony scrambled onto the bed, excitement written all over his face. Liz took her time lubing up the strap-on before shoving it into him. He let out a sharp cry of pleasure.

"Yes, master," Tony groaned. "I've been such a bad boy."

Liz grabbed a chain, looping it around his neck. Tugging firmly, she said, "Come on, my dog. I'm taking you for a walk."

She led him to a chair and sat down, leaning back. Tony stood in front of her, his hands sliding up her body. He cupped her chest, his tongue circling her nipples as she moaned. Liz grabbed his head, guiding it lower.

Tony obeyed, his tongue working its way up and down, in and out, until Liz climaxed, her cries filling the room.

Afterward, they jumped into the shower together, washing away the intensity of the night. Without a word, Liz gathered her things and left, leaving Tony standing in the doorway, still breathless and dazed.

At 5:30 AM, Liz stumbled into the house, heading straight to her room. Without bothering to change, she collapsed onto her bed and passed out. Moments later, Sue woke up and shuffled down the hall. On her way to the bathroom, she paused at Liz's room, grabbed a blanket, and gently threw it over her. Smiling to herself, Sue continued to the bathroom.

After a refreshing shower, Sue got ready for the day. She applied her makeup carefully, slipped into a crisp blue-and-white blouse paired with a sleek pencil skirt, and stepped into her red-bottom Louis Vuitton's by the front door. Feeling polished and confident, she grabbed her keys and headed to work.

As soon as Sue walked into the office, her boss called out, "Sue, can you come to my office, please?"

Heart pounding, Sue replied, "What's going on? Am I in trouble?"

Her boss chuckled. "No, not at all. I actually have good news. I wanted to tell you in person— you're being promoted to top editor!"

Sue's jaw dropped. "Wait—does that mean I get my own office?"

Her boss smiled. "Yes, it does. Come on, I'll show you."

Sue could barely contain her excitement as she followed her boss down the hall. When she stepped into her new office, she was greeted by a massive stack of papers on her desk. Laughing, she said, "Looks like you've loaded me up with work already."

Her boss grinned. "You're amazing at what you do. I know you'll handle it by tomorrow."

Sue sank into her new office chair, propped her legs on the desk, and snapped a selfie. She sent the picture to Kevin via JPay Messenger with the caption:

"Hey Kevin, still waiting on those divorce papers you never sent back. Oh, and how do you like the pic? I'm doing great, by the way."

Moments later, her desk phone rang. The voice on the other end was deep and angry. "I'll show you a damn divorce," Kevin growled.

Sue snapped back, "Kevin, is that a threat?" She hung up before he could respond.

Later, a knock at the door broke her concentration. She opened it and immediately screamed,

"Oh my God, Mike! I haven't seen you in ages!"

Mike pulled her into a tight hug and whispered smoothly, "I've missed you, friend."

She ushered him into her office, and he looked around, taking in her setup. "Damn, you're doing your big one, mama!"

"And I am!" Sue replied, laughing as they bantered.

Her phone buzzed again. She held up a finger to Mike and answered, "Hello?" "Hey, Sue, I haven't heard from you in hours," Liz said.

Sue sighed. "You saw me just this morning when I was rushing out. What's up?"

"I was just wondering if you're coming home soon. I've got something for you," Liz replied.

Sue hesitated. "I'll think about it. I've got a lot of work to do, but I'll let you know when I'm on my way."

Mike raised an eyebrow. "Who was that with the soft voice?"

Sue rolled her eyes. "That was Liz. And let me tell you something—girl's been messing around with this guy, Tony. He's into being dominated, and you know Liz loves to experiment." Mike's eyes widened. "Wait—Tony? Girl, you're not serious!"

Sue leaned in, lowering her voice. "I swear. But don't say I told you. You know I'm not trying to be messy."

Mike pulled his chair closer, grinning. "Tell me more."

Sue smirked, ready to spill the tea, but before she could say anything else, Mike stood up. "You better be ready tonight," he said.

"Ready for what?" Sue asked.

"We're going out to the club. And you're bringing Liz with you," Mike replied with a wink.

Sue laughed. "Fine! I'll tell her to get it together."

As Mike left her office, Sue grabbed her phone and texted Liz:

"I don't care what you've got going on tonight, but you're coming out with me and Mike. Be ready."

At 2:30 p.m., Sue called Mike. "Are you picking me up? If so, I'll make sure I'm ready," she asked.

Mike replied, "Well, you and Liz can ride with me. I just need y'all hoes to be ready." "Mike, I'm not a hoe," Sue shot back.

"Hold on, someone's calling me on the other line," Mike said, switching over. "Hello?"

A firm, deep voice answered, "Hey Mike, you miss me?" Mike rolled his eyes. "William, I don't. What do you want?" "You're still bitter as hell, huh?" William teased.

"Like I said, what do you want?" Mike snapped.

Before William could answer, a voice in the background interrupted. "Bae, who are you on the phone with? I'm hungry," the aggressive tone cut through.

"William!" Mike yelled. "So you call me, but you're talking to everybody else in the background? Some things never change."

William hung up abruptly but followed with a text: You're lucky I'm on my way to therapy, or I'd come over and fuck shit up.

Frustrated, Mike decided to go to therapy himself. He walked into Dr. Guess's office, where the doctor greeted him calmly.

"Hello, Mike. What brings you in today? Glad you're taking advantage of our walk-in appointments."

Mike collapsed onto the couch. "Doc, I need help! I'm two seconds from going to William's house and burning it to the ground!"

Dr. Guess leaned forward, his voice steady. "Now, Mike, do you really think that's worth going to jail for?"

Mike inhaled deeply, following the breathing exercises Dr. Guess demonstrated, before finally venting. "I'm really trying to get over this man, Doc. I haven't seen William in months, but when I heard that feminine voice in the background, I lost it. How can he move on so fast when I'm stuck?"

"When you love someone, it takes time to let go," Dr. Guess replied. "But I'm glad to hear you're going out tonight with friends.

That's a good first step. If you feel overwhelmed, remember the breathing exercises."

After the session, Mike headed home to get ready. He sent Liz and Sue a group text: Hey, lovebugs. Be ready in two. Both responded with popping bottle emojis.

Once home, Mike sat at his dining table, his head in his hands. "You've got this, Mike," he told himself in the bathroom mirror as he trimmed his hair. He turned on upbeat music, belting out lyrics as he jumped into the shower. Afterward, he slipped on his sexy lace underwear, pulled up skinny jeans that hugged his frame, and slid into a fishnet shirt. A few sprays of cologne later, he was out the door.

At 9 p.m., Mike pulled up to Liz and Sue's house, honking four times. Liz opened the door. "Mike, you don't have to do all that damn blowing!" she scolded.

Sue and Liz climbed into the car. Mike shook a bag of weed at Sue. "You rolling this or not?"

Liz snatched the bag. "Let's get high as hell!"

The three shared a blunt as they drove to the club, laughing and feeling the buzz.

Inside, Mike noticed a booth with his name on it. As they walked over, Liz nudged Sue and pointed to the bar. William stood there with a woman in a tight black dress and Air Jordans.

Mike tried to ignore them. "What are you drinking, ladies?" he asked, forcing a smile.

Liz smirked. "You already know."

"Tito's and lemonade for me!" Sue chimed in.

Mike went to order, but Liz stopped him, whispering in his ear, "Look who's at the bar." Mike glanced over, irritation flashing across his face.

"William," he muttered under his breath. "Y'all go grab the drinks. I need a minute."

At the bar, William greeted Liz and Sue. "Oh, hey, my girls! Let me guess—you're with Mike?"

"Yep, and we're not about to entertain your bullshit," Liz said sharply.

"Whatever. Let me introduce you to my girlfriend." William gestured to the woman beside him.

"This is Precious."

Precious extended her hand. "Hi! Nice to meet you."

Liz smiled politely. "Cute haircut."

"Thanks," Precious replied. "William did it."

Sue snorted. "Oh, he never does my hair, and we're supposed to be friends."

William interjected, "Girl, you never come to my shop!"

Back at the booth, Mike sipped his drink. "What took y'all so long?"

Sue smirked. "We were being nosey."

Mike rolled his eyes. "Fuck William and that bald-headed hoe he's with."

"Enough with the negativity!" Sue said, pulling them to the dance floor. "This is my jam!"

The three danced through the crowd, losing themselves in the music until William appeared. "Hey, friend," he said.

Mike spun around. "Boy, don't 'friend' me. Where's your girl?"

"Don't worry about her," William snapped. "I don't know why you're so bitter."

Before he could finish, Mike swung his fist, connecting with William's jaw. The two tumbled to the ground, fists flying. Precious ran up, trying to pull Mike off, but Liz and Sue intervened, dragging Precious by her hair and delivering an uppercut. Chaos erupted until security broke up the brawl, shutting the club down.

Outside, William stumbled out with Precious. "This is your fault!" she shouted. "I told you I didn't want drama tonight!"

"You're messing up my buzz, woman," William mumbled, brushing past her.

Meanwhile, Mike, Liz, and Sue jumped into the car, still hyped. "We beat her ass!" Liz cheered.

"You didn't have to do her like that," Mike laughed mischievously, dropping them off before heading home.

As he pulled into his driveway, he spotted William on his porch. "What the hell are you doing here?" Mike barked.

"I'm sorry," William cried. "Please, can I come in?"

Reluctantly, Mike opened the door. Inside, William confessed, "Precious is pregnant. I'm going to be a father."

Mike froze. "Are you serious? Why are you even here?"

William leaned in, kissing him passionately. Old feelings flared, and before

Mike knew it, they were in his bedroom, stripping each other's clothes. Mike trailed kisses down William's back, teasing him before their passion took over.

As William's phone buzzed repeatedly, Mike glanced at it. Precious's name flashed angrily across the screen.

William rushed out of Mike's house, half-dressed, and jumped into an Uber. On the phone with Precious, he tried to steady his voice as she screamed into the receiver.

"Precious, you need to calm down. I'm on my way home," William said firmly.

"Where are you?" Precious snapped. "You should be here with me!" "You told me not to come home!" William shouted back, frustrated.

"You would've come home any other time," she replied before abruptly hanging up.

When William arrived home, he stepped inside to find Precious yelling and pacing the living room, her voice trembling with fury.

"Where the hell have you been?" she demanded.

William froze, looking around the house with a mixture of confusion and apprehension. Ignoring her for a moment, he walked to their bedroom. As he entered, his eyes fell on a condom wrapper sitting on the bed near the pillow. His stomach sank.

Precious followed him into the room, her footsteps heavy with tension. She stopped and fell silent as William turned to face her, his expression a storm of anger and disbelief.

"So, you brought someone here?" William asked, his voice rising. "That's why you didn't want me to come home last night?"

Precious crossed her arms defensively, her voice barely above a whisper. "It doesn't matter."

William turned and stormed into the kitchen, trying to gather his thoughts. He grabbed a pan and placed it on the stove, pulling out ingredients from the fridge. "We'll talk about it over lunch," he said, his voice tight with restraint.

Precious appeared in the doorway, her tone suddenly soft. "Baby, do you need help?"

"Yeah," William muttered. "Hand me a couple of those potatoes."

As she moved toward the counter, William noticed her slight limp. Concern flickered across his face. "Are you okay?" he asked, studying her.

"No," Precious admitted, her voice tinged with pain. "I'm sore from the fight last night. We got jumped, and I might need to go to the hospital to make sure everything's okay with the baby."

William's brows frowned, worry clouding his features. "You sure that's from the fight?" he asked bluntly. "Or was it from the guy you had over last night?"

Precious's face hardened as she turned on him, her voice rising. "That's what I'm talking about, William! You keep bringing up last night, but you're the one who stayed out. So why does it matter if I was with someone or not?"

William stood at the sink, shaking his head silently. He plated their food and set the table, trying to push the tension aside. Precious sat across from him, her demeanor softening as she glanced at the meal. "Everything looks great," she murmured.

As they ate, Precious finally spoke. "William, I'm not used to dating a bisexual man. This is all different for me. Every time you step out, I have to worry about women and men. Plus, it's your fault we got into that altercation last night. You were drunk and belligerent, worrying about your ex."

William's phone rang, cutting through the tense conversation. Precious shot him a glare as he held up a finger to signal her to wait. He answered, his tone shifting instantly to one of excitement.

"Tree! I haven't talked to you in a minute. What's going on?"

"Nothing much," Tree replied. "How about you?"

William smiled. "I'm sitting here with my lovely baby mama, eating lunch."

On speakerphone, Tree greeted Precious. "Hey, baby mama!"

"Hey, Tree," Precious replied, her tone still laced with irritation.

William filled Tree in on the chaos of the previous night. Tree sighed. "You know Liz is a messy ass bitch, right? Oh, and Mike? Yeah, he's definitely trouble."

William laughed. "No doubt about that."

Tree changed the subject. "Hey, I'm throwing a birthday party, and I want everyone to come.

Even Liz."

Precious scoffed loudly at the mention of Liz, pushing her plate away. "Are you serious,

William? You're just going to pretend everything is fine after last night?"

William frowned, lowering the phone. "Precious, we can talk about this later." Tree's voice cut in, amused. "Oh, is this about Liz? She still running her mouth?"

Precious leaned forward, glaring at the phone. "Tree, if you're such a good friend, why don't you tell William to stop entertaining Liz's drama? She's always stirring up problems."

"Precious," William warned, his tone sharp.

Tree hesitated. "I mean, Precious has a point, but y'all need to work this out. I'm just trying to throw a party, not referee your mess."

William exhaled, pinching the bridge of his nose. "Tree, I'll call you back later. I need to deal with this." He ended the call and turned to Precious, his expression a mixture of exhaustion and frustration.

"What do you want from me, Precious? Do you want me to grovel, apologize for things I didn't even do? You're acting like I'm the one who cheated!"

"Maybe because you're never here when I need you!" she fired back, standing from the table.

William's voice rose, his emotions spilling over. "I'm out trying to keep us afloat, Precious! Do you think I enjoy running to Mike's house or working extra shifts just to come home to this?"

Precious blinked, her anger faltering as tears welled in her eyes. "You don't get it. I'm scared,

William. I'm scared of losing you, of raising this baby alone, of not being enough for you."

William stared at her, his own anger dissipating as her words sank in. He stood and walked over to her, placing his hands gently on her shoulders. "Precious, I'm here. I know it's not perfect, and I know I mess up, but I'm trying. For you, for us, and for this baby."

She sniffled, nodding slightly. "I don't want to lose you."

"You're not going to," William said firmly. "But we've got to trust each other. If we don't, this'll never work."

Precious nodded again, wiping her tears. "Okay. I'll try. But you've got to meet me halfway, William."

"I will," he promised.

The tension in the room lifted slightly, leaving a fragile peace between them. As William reached for her hand, his phone buzzed again. He ignored it, pulling Precious into a hug instead.

For the first time in what felt like weeks, they stood together in silence, holding onto the hope that things could get better.

William took Precious to the hospital, where they sat in the waiting room for about an hour. Precious grew increasingly impatient, shifting uncomfortably in her seat. William put his arm around her, trying to console her.

"It should be almost time," he said softly.

Finally, they called Precious to the back. The doctor greeted them and asked, "What's going on?"

Nervously, Precious replied, "I don't know. I'm just in so much pain, and every time I use the bathroom, there's blood."

The doctor wasted no time and started running several tests. Precious lay on the hospital bed, clutching William's hand while they waited for the results. William held her hand tightly, offering silent support as the minutes dragged on.

When the doctor returned, he wore a solemn expression. "Based on the test results, you're having a miscarriage," he said gently. Both Precious and William froze, their breaths catching in their throats.

"But," the doctor continued, "as we looked at the ultrasound, we saw you still have two babies.

It seems you were originally pregnant with triplets, and you're only five weeks along."

Precious and William stared at him, stunned and scared. The news was overwhelming.

The doctor's tone grew firmer. "You'll need to go on bed rest for the next few weeks to give your body the best chance to stabilize."

Precious couldn't hold it in anymore and broke down into tears. William quickly grabbed her clothes and wiped the tears from her face, whispering reassurances to her, though his own face was filled with worry.

Meanwhile, Liz was lounging on her couch, laughing over wine with Sue. The air was casual, but Sue's face grew serious as she brought up the incident from the other night.

"Liz," Sue began hesitantly, "I've been feeling awful about the fight. I was so drunk, and I didn't mean to go off on Precious like that."

Liz's laugh was sharp and cutting. "Girl, stop feeling bad for that bitch. We did what needed to be done. She was running her mouth all night, acting like she owned the place." Her voice hardened. "Precious got exactly what she deserved."

Sue raised an eyebrow but smirked. "You're such a savage, Liz."

"Anyway," Liz continued, sipping her drink, "Tree called me. She's having a birthday party. I'm thinking about bringing Tony."

Sue's eyes widened, her laugh bursting out uncontrollably. "Tony? To *Tree's* party? You are such a messy bitch—but damn, I love it."

Later, Liz grabbed her phone and texted Tony with her signature confidence: *Hey Tony, I miss you.*

The reply came swiftly:

Hello, gorgeous.

A sly smile tugged at Liz's lips as she typed her next message:

You should come to this birthday party with me. Full disclosure, it's my ex's party.

There was a pause before Tony responded.

I appreciate you being upfront. I'd love to go. What colors are we wearing?

Liz's heart raced as she typed back, □□ *I'll let you pick, gorgeous.*

Tony's reply came fast, smooth as ever:

Red would look amazing on that body of yours.

Liz smirked at the screen, her mind already plotting. *Talk to you later,* she typed before tossing her phone aside, her thoughts drifting to the chaos she knew was about to unfold.

Liz picked up her phone and called Tree.

"Hey, Tree. Is it okay if I bring a plus one?"

Tree answered with a slight hesitation. "Yeah, as long as there's no damn drama."

Liz chuckled. "I'm not on that. You invited me, so I want to come, support, and start fresh."

Tree sighed, then hesitantly added, "Liz, please don't start anything with my girlfriend. I know she answered my phone rudely."

Liz smirked. "Oh, so you must be cheating on her too, huh?"

Tree groaned. "Come on, Liz, we just agreed on a fresh start. Now you're being nosy about my relationship?"

Liz let the silence linger for a moment before Tree brushed it off. "Alright, Liz, I'll see you at my birthday party.

Sue's phone rang, cutting through the quiet hum of her living room. She picked it up, her voice calm but guarded. "Hello, I accept the collect call."

Kevin's voice came through, gruff and direct. "What up, Sue? I signed those divorce papers.

Your attorney should have them by now."

A wave of relief washed over Sue, and she couldn't contain her excitement.

"Thank you so much! I can finally be free from you."

Kevin chuckled bitterly. "Lucky you, I guess. Anyway, I'm getting out of the rehabilitation facility tomorrow. I was wondering if I could stay with you."

Sue's demeanor shifted instantly. Her voice was sharp and unwavering. "Nigga, hell to the naw. You're toxic as hell. Good day, Kevin." Without waiting for a response, she hung up the phone, her hands trembling with frustration.

Trying to compose herself, Sue walked into the dining room, where Liz sat scrolling through her phone, casually shopping for an outfit. Liz glanced up, her brow furrowing as she read the tension on Sue's face.

"What's wrong, girl?" Liz asked, her tone laced with concern.

Sue exhaled sharply, dropping into a chair. "Kevin's coming home next week. He had the audacity to ask if he could stay here."

Liz's face twisted in disbelief. "Hell naw. He better call his boy Mike or somebody else 'cause it ain't happening here." She quickly shifted the mood, flashing a mischievous grin. "Anyway, girl,

I'm wearing my fishnet bodysuit, thigh-high boots, and my fur coat to Tree's party."

Sue smirked, appreciating the quick change of subject. "That's gonna be so cute! I'm wearing my sleek slacks with my see-through floaty blouse."

Liz nodded approvingly. "Did you order some shoes yet? If not, let me add it to my cart so it'll be here tomorrow."

Sue perked up, her frustration melting away. "You know what? I'm gonna wear my all-gold YSL. It's time to step out in style."

The two friends laughed, the tension from earlier dissipating as they leaned into the comfort of their bond. They spent the rest of the night chilling, planning outfits, and talking about everything *but* Kevin.

****

Tree's Birthday Party

On Saturday at 9:30 PM, Tree's birthday party was in full swing. As she walked into the establishment, heads turned she was stunning. Her long dreads were pinned up, and she wore a silver sparkly pantsuit that shimmered under the lights. On her feet were black Louis Vuitton gym shoes adorned with silver spikes and red bottoms. The DJ had been playing birthday songs back to back, setting the mood for the night.

Guests began to arrive, filling the venue with excitement. Tree, wanting to make a grand entrance, sat in the back, watching the room come to life.

Mike stepped inside, looking around in approval. "This is nice," he muttered to himself before spotting Tree. His eyes widened she looked breathtaking. Shocked by her beauty, he made his way toward her.

Tree smirked. "Just so you know, I invited Will and his girlfriend, Precious."

Mike's face instantly shifted to irritation. "Tree... I knew you were gonna invite them. You guys are friends, so I get it. But don't worry I'll behave myself tonight."

Tree arched an eyebrow. "You better. I look way too good to be breaking up a fight."

Mike chuckled. "Relax, we're cool... for now."

As the party continued, Sue walked in, looking around with approval. "Wow, this is nice," she said, not immediately noticing Tree standing nearby with Mike.

Tree called out, "Hey Sue! Thanks for coming. We 'bout to turn this bitch up!"

The DJ switched up the vibe, playing a local artist's song that everyone knew. Without hesitation, Tree grabbed Mike's hand. "Come on, let's hit the dance floor like we used to back in the day."

Sue, Mike, and Tree lost themselves in the music, dancing hard until sweat dripped from their foreheads.

In the middle of it all, Tree's girlfriend walked over. "Hey, bae," she said, catching Tree's attention.

Tree turned around and smiled before introducing her. "This is Mike, and this is Sue."

Mike's eyes scanned Tree's girlfriend from head to toe before calmly saying, "Tree... this who you messing with?"

Tree rolled her eyes and playfully hit his shoulder. "Boy, stop! Don't look at my girl like that."

Mike smirked and shook his head. "You know I don't do tuna."

Both he and Tree burst into laughter, while Sue watched with mild amusement.

Sue then turned to Tree's girlfriend. "What's your name?"

"Hi, I'm Jess. Nice to meet you," she responded.

Sue nodded but then quickly added, "So... you the one that was getting smart with my best friend, Liz?"

Jess's whole demeanor shifted. She crossed her arms, giving Liz a once-over as Liz stepped closer.

"What's up? We got a problem?" Liz asked, ready for whatever was about to unfold.

Jess turned to Tree. "Baby, you need to check your friends before I do."

Before the tension could escalate, Tony walked up and hugged Liz, whispering in her ear,

"Baby, please play nice today. We're here to have a good time."

Liz sighed but softened, wrapping her arms around Tony and rubbing his head affectionately. Meanwhile, Tree noticed the interaction and walked over with a look of irritation.

"Tony, Tony, Tony," Tree called out. "I see you got my leftovers. Hope you enjoy and get full."

Tony shook his head and chuckled. "Why you worried about us? We happy over here."

Liz chimed in, "Come on now, Tree, this is your birthday party, and you're already stirring up drama. We came to have a good time."

Tree exhaled deeply, rolling her eyes. "Ugh... yeah, you right."

The music picked up again, and the night continued, full of energy, laughter, and the occasional side-eye.

Just as the drama started to settle, the DJ grabbed the mic.

"Ayo, everybody, make some noise for the birthday girl, Tree!"

The crowd erupted in cheers, and Tree threw her hands up, flashing a big, confident smile. The tension from earlier melted away—at least for now.

Sue nudged Tree playfully. "Come on, let's get you on stage. It's your night."

Tree hesitated for a second, her eyes flickering toward Jess, Mike, and the rest of the crew, but then she shook it off. Tonight was about her, not old drama or petty stares.

She strutted toward the DJ booth as a new track dropped, the bass vibrating through the floor. The spotlight hit her, making the silver in her pantsuit sparkle like diamonds.

Grabbing the mic, she grinned. "Alright, y'all know what it is! We 'bout to turn this up another level. If you came to celebrate with me, I wanna see y'all on this dance floor!"

The crowd roared in approval as the beat switched to an anthem that had everyone hyped. Drinks were raised, bodies swayed, and for that moment, nothing else mattered.

As the party roared on, Tree locked eyes with Jess, who gave her a knowing smirk. Somewhere across the room, Mike was still side-eyeing her relationship choices, and Liz and Tony were wrapped up in their own world.

Mike walked over to the DJ booth, grabbed the mic, and called out, "Tree, you know we can't end the night without your gift!"

With a grin, he stepped outside to his car, popped the trunk, and pulled out a glittery box with Tree's name written all over it. Returning to the mic, he announced, "Tree, I have a special gift for you, and I want you to open it in front of everyone. It's from me and the rest of us."

Tree's eyes widened in surprise as she walked over to the box. She carefully started unwrapping it, pausing to admire the wrapping. "I really don't want to rip this paper—it's so cute!" she laughed.

But as she tore into it, her expression shifted to confusion. Inside the big box was just a small envelope buried in confetti paper. She let out a chuckle. "Oh my God! A huge box for this tiny thing? Thank you anyway, Mike."

Before she could say more, the entire party erupted in unison, "OPEN IT!"

With a mix of curiosity and excitement, she tore open the envelope—and froze. Inside was a check for $500,000.

Her hands trembled as she stared at it, her emotions swirling between shock, joy, and disbelief. Before she could process it, Mike's voice boomed through the speakers.

"Tree, we all came together and pitched in for your gift. This check is for you to finally open the car rental business you've been struggling to launch."

The room exploded in cheers as Tree's eyes filled with tears, overwhelmed by the love and generosity surrounding her.

Tree exhaled, feeling the weight of it all, but pushed it aside. Tonight was hers. Whatever came next—well, she'd deal with that when the sun came up.

With a deep breath, she stepped off the stage and let herself get lost in the night.

****

Reflections

After leaving Tony's place, Liz took a deep breath, allowing herself a rare moment of reflection. She had come so far—survived so much. Instead of diving headfirst into another relationship, she finally recognized what she truly deserved: peace, healing, and the space to rediscover herself before giving her heart to someone else.

As she drove home, the city lights stretched into golden streaks against the night sky. Her body still hummed from the night's electricity, but her mind wrestled with a deeper question—had she been chasing love, or running from herself?

For once, she craved something more than passion. Clarity. No more losing herself in tangled emotions. No more falling into the same patterns. It was time to choose Liz.

Yet, despite her newfound resolve, a part of her still ached for Tony. That soft, vulnerable piece of her wanted to let go, to sink into the warmth they shared. Only they truly understood the unspoken language of their connection. She carried deep scars from her past—Tree had left wounds that still lingered—but Tony accepted her, all of her. He saw the dominant, unshakable side of her, the part of her that refused to be broken. And he loved it.

She had never been with a man before, yet with him, she found herself embracing something unexpected—his gentleness. His softness didn't weaken her; it invited her in, showing her a different kind of strength.

Maybe she wasn't ready to fall in love again. But for the first time in a long while, she wasn't afraid to feel.

****

Sue's Power Move

Sue was sipping her morning coffee when her phone rang. She eyed the unknown number, debating whether to answer. With a sigh, she picked up.

"This is a call from Bright Horizon Rehabilitation Center. Do you accept the charges?"

Her stomach clenched. "Kevin"

She took a slow breath, steadying herself. "Yeah, I accept."

Kevin's voice was softer than she remembered stripped of cockiness, free of bitterness. Just quiet, almost hesitant.

"Sue... I signed the divorce papers. Your attorney should have them by now." Relief swept through her. "Thank you," she said, meaning it.

A pause stretched between them.

"I also wanted to say I'm sorry," Kevin admitted. "For everything. I'm finally getting the help I should've gotten years ago."

Sue frowned, caught off guard by his sincerity. "What changed?"

Kevin let out a dry laugh. "Losing everything. Hitting rock bottom. The fire, the cheating, the way I treated you, it all caught up to me. I had to face myself, and I didn't like what I saw."

She let his words settle. For years, she had dreamed of hearing him take accountability. Now that he had, she didn't feel the urge to lash out, to make him hurt the way she had. She just felt... at peace.

"I'm glad you're getting help, Kevin," she said finally. "But that doesn't change anything for me.

I've moved on."

"I know," he admitted. "I don't deserve another chance. But I hope, someday, you'll think of me and remember something good, too."

She considered that for a moment, then gave a small, knowing smile. "Maybe."

As she ended the call, she exhaled deeply, the weight of the past finally lifting. Kevin's chapter in her life was officially closed—but this time, on her terms. No anger, no regret. Just closure.

****

To Growth and Success

That Sunday afternoon, Liz, Mike, and Sue lounged on the patio, sipping mimosas under the golden summer sun. For the first time in a long time, there was no drama, no lies—just laughter and peace.

"We've been through hell," Liz admitted, swirling her drink. "But at least we've got each other."

Mike clinked his glass against hers. "And no matter what happens next, we'll always have each other's backs."

He leaned back, stretching with satisfaction. "I feel so relieved, y'all. I'm officially done with therapy. It's like I have a whole new outlook on life. I feel... refreshed."

Liz smirked. "You do look refreshed—skin all clear and shit."

Sue chuckled, reaching under her chair and pulling out two gift bags. "Speaking of feeling good, I got something for you two. I think you'll enjoy it."

Mike grabbed his bag and immediately started screaming with excitement. "Yes! Receipts don't lie!"

Sue beamed. "I finally released my book, and guess what? It made the New York Times Best Sellers list."

Liz gasped, her eyes welling up. "Oh my God, Sue! I'm so happy for you. These are happy tears, just so you know."

Wiping her face, she took a deep breath and grinned mischievously. "Since everybody's sharing good news, I have some too. But before that, I got a little tea to spill."

Mike and Sue exchanged knowing looks and shook their heads. "Here we go," they said in unison.

Liz leaned in, lowering her voice like she was about to share the juiciest gossip. "Did y'all hear about Precious and William? They had twin girls."

Mike's eyes widened. "I knew she was pregnant, but twins? That's wild. Good for them."

Sue raised an eyebrow. "Okay, but what's your tea? Since you're spilling everybody else's."

Liz smirked, reaching into her purse. With a dramatic pause, she placed a pregnancy test on the table.

"Me and Tony are having one of your nieces or nephews."

Mike's jaw dropped. "That's why you weren't drinking all afternoon!"

Liz winked. "You know I love my mimosas. Had to keep the secret somehow."

Before the excitement could settle, Liz's phone buzzed. She glanced at it and grinned. "Oh, and guess who else is winning right now? Tree just launched her own car rental company!"

Sue's eyes lit up. "For real? That's huge!"

Mike clapped his hands together. "That's what I'm talking about! Black excellence all around!"

Liz nodded. "She's already getting bookings. I told her we gotta celebrate soon."

Sue raised her glass. "To growth, success, and new beginnings."

Liz and Mike lifted their glasses, clinking them together. "To us."

Laughter erupted between them, the joy of the moment sealing their bond even deeper. No matter what twists life had in store, they had each other and that was all that mattered.

Acknowledgements

I want to express my deepest gratitude to my close family and friends for encouraging me to pursue and complete this project. Special thanks to my late mother Latrina Gilchrist, and to all my ancestors who came before her. Their sacrifices, wisdom, and love have laid the foundation for the strength and determination I carry with me today. This project is as much a testament to their legacy as it is to my own journey."

Books By This Author

Fiction

- Secrets, Surprises, and Late Nights

Coloring Books

- Loving You Through Our Affirmations: Couples Edition

- Loving You Through Our Affirmations: Mother & Son Edition

- Loving You Through Our Affirmations: Daddy & Daughter Edition

- Color Your Damn Feelings: A No Judge Coloring Book for Real Life Emotions

About the Author

Wydale D. Gilchrist began his writing journey in 2018, driven by a lifelong passion for storytelling and a mind that had been overflowing with ideas for years. For a long time, he kept his stories to himself but eventually realized they were meant to be shared.

Writing is more than an outlet for Wydale; it's a way to connect, inspire, and bring hidden narratives to life. Through his work, he explores emotion, identity, relationships, and moments that often go unspoken, creating stories that feel honest, intimate, and real.

When he's not writing, Wydale continues to create work that encourages reflection, expression, and connection across different forms of storytelling.